3032

Onto The Entangled Paths

By

Arjun Malhotra

From all my heart and mind, my first brain-heart child, to you.

Contents

PART 1
I Thought I Knew
(Marcus Robinson)

Introduction

'Tough times... It is tough to be in a lonely place and no one with you. Work, work, and work is what you have. But this time it is important. It is for our planet.

It seems the world has come to an end. We don't have a drop of water to drink or even oxygen to breathe. Crops are dying and people too. I just want everything to be as it was, or where it all started. But I can't do that because neither am I the one to decide nor do I have the powers to. I am Marcus Robinson; this is the planet Earth and the year is 3032. I am far away from the city, at a place out of everyone's reach. I am in a secret laboratory. It is a place that could maybe the safest place on the planet right now. Especially built for us; a group of 100 members consisting of experts from all over the world and we are here to save the planet or find a new one.'

Chapter One

THE MEETING

It was the second meeting after we were called up here and this time it seemed to be an important one. I thought that in this meeting we would be asked what progress was made so far. But that wasn't the truth, or you may say that the reality was entirely different.

I saw other faces in the hall, and they seemed very sad and disappointed in themselves. Maybe because the research we have done till now was not up to the mark or didn't give us any clue. After a few minutes, we entered the hall and heard a voice coming from behind; It was the president of NASA along with the presidents of ISRO, SpaceX, and many other organisations. He had a strong build, deep brown eyes, and short black hair. Every time I had seen him, walking around in the hallway, or coming to check on us almost every day, he seemed to carry a lot of pride on his chest. Maybe it was ego. I can't tell for sure. With a smile always plastered on his face, no matter how bad the situations got. Seeing that, I concluded that maybe he is narcissistic. He always seems so full of himself. And in these upsetting conditions, 'Why the f*** does he always smile?'

They entered the hall while everyone else stared at them. 'I would like to welcome everyone present here and thank you all for working day and night to save this, to save our planet.' He said (that smile still not leaving his face) 'On behalf of NASA and other organisations, we have decided that Earth can no longer be our home planet. After many unsuccessful attempts to find life on Mars; we have seen that there is no place for us in this galaxy. Therefore, we have now thought of migrating. Migrating to some other galaxy. The star we have found is 40 light-years away. 'Trapped 1'; this star was found a thousand years ago, but we were not able to do anything then because we didn't have the required resources. The star has 7 planets revolving around it and as we know that all the planets come from the living zone. It is presumed that all planets are rocky. The most suitable planet we have found is the 5th planet in the series. Also Trapped 1 only receives 50% of the heat from the sun, which means that there will be a little cold out there. So don't forget to carry sweaters.' He laughed. 'We have also got to know that there is water on those planets but we still don't know if it's acidic or not. The 7 planets are completely rocky. Earlier we had also sent signals to that planet but haven't received any responses. We still believe life exists there. So, we are going to send some of our best members to that galaxy. Now I am going to call out the names of the Top 5 chosen by us. The names are: Dr. Vishnu Patel from ISRO, Dr. Makoto Stewart from JAXA, Dr. Delano Lambert from EESA, Dr. Jay Evans from SpaceX, and at the last, the leader of the group Dr. Marcus Robinson from NASA. Congratulations to all the members for being assigned to the biggest mission ever undertaken in the history of this universe. Now I would like to hear a big round of applause for all the members while they come here.' Claps surrounded us while we stepped forward and with this the meeting finished.

Chapter Two

MYSTERIES

This decision gave me a tough day. It took my sleep away from me. I had nothing to do, but think about what just happened. There was no happiness on my face for becoming the first person to do such a mission. Only which showed up were despondency and a grave fear. Something was irritating me. It was like a voice, which was telling me to stay and not go as if I was not going to find anything there or the mission could take my life. But I was ignoring it because I had no choice instead of doing what I was told to do. I have followed orders all my life. I have never defied them. Whatever they told me to do, I did. So now, disobeying them would make no sense.

It was around 9:00 p.m., I was in my room laying down on my bed and thinking about if the decision I made was worth it. And suddenly the doorbell rang. I shouted, 'who's there' (not in a good mood).

'Hey, Mark it's Stewart. I have something to talk about; something you would like to hear.'

'Door open,' I said, and the door opened. I got up while Stewart came in. I went to the sofa with Stewart, and we sat down.

Stewart had always been a good friend to me since we came here. He always helped me through my tough times and never left me alone. He treated me like I was his family. He was always flippant in the beginning, but as time passed by, it was like fun was nowhere to be seen.

He held my hand into his. It felt like there was some problem because he always did that when there was upsetting news.

He spoke 'Mark, I know you are feeling strained right now and I don't want to disturb you. But I have heard that they will put our lives on trial.'

I smiled 'I know that too, there's nothing new about it.'

'No, there is. I have heard that the spacecraft's damaged. Some of the parts are damaged and now it's too late to try and repair them. They can't be repaired now.'

I suddenly stood up in anger 'What the F***! We must do something. That's not going to work at all. We must stand up to them.'

'No, It's just not that simple. It is not going to work.'

'But why?'

'Because we are just five, and there are many more who could be selected instead of us. I know that you wouldn't want anyone else to die.'

As I was listening to what Stewart had to say I was getting more and more terrified of everything. As if my whole life was flashing in front of my eyes. I was thinking about my parents, siblings, cousins, friends, and everyone I held close. It was a feeling that everything was going to end, and I would be left with nothing. The land I stand upon, the air I breathe, the water I drink, and the people I love. Everything will be going away.

'So, what do we do now,' I asked. He asked me for a day to think about the resolution and I had no choice other than agreeing to what he just said.

This conversation took my sleep away completely. As opposed to looking to start a good day, I was hoping to be able to see another one.

Chapter Three

UNEXPECTED SURPRISES

I didn't wake up the next day because I didn't sleep. I was awake the whole night, thinking about everything that had happened.

It was 9:00 in the morning and I rushed to the door of Stewart's room. When the door opened and I saw Stewart, I asked the first and only question that was on my mind 'Did you think about something?' He couldn't answer me anything. Not even a single word came out of his mouth. I was very angry and afraid. He promised me. He told me that he would find a solution. He asked me to calm down and wait for him to think of something, yet he didn't do anything.

'Stewart, you told me to wait and now I can't wait anymore. I just don't have that much patience. I just can't wait and see us die with the expectations of billions of people on us. We are responsible for each and everything which will happen to them, and I won't let those billions of hopes and the entire existence of humankind vanish. I don't need any help from you now, I will do what I want and what's best for everyone.'

After that, I walked away, and Stewart remained quiet.

***

It was the third meeting which was organised for the selected ones only. It was the next day after the second one but it made sense to have it just the next day because time was too short to wait. And this time I knew what I had to do. Just before the meeting was going to start and NASA's president was going to say anything I stood up in anger 'What the hell are you going to say? Huh?' Everyone started looking at me with surprise. 'You bitches are going to put our lives in danger. I know that you people know that there is a problem in the spacecraft but aren't doing anything about it cause it can't be fixed now. Have you lost your goddamn minds?' Just before I was going to say anything else the president interrupted me, 'Do you have any better plan? We are not fools here, we have given this a lot of thought and in the end, we decided to do so. We have taken this decision after hours of discussion.' 'Hmmm, so this fool proof plan to death is discussed at length. Would you please tell me what have you premeditated?' I gave the president a sarcastic smile but he was in no mood 'So now that everyone has calmed down, I would like to start the meeting. This mission is going to be the biggest mission ever known to mankind. We know that traveling at the speed of light is certainly impossible and I would sound insane if I said that we could do so. So, we have decided that we will be using the hibernation technique. Now the problem arises that if hibernation is used it would take a long time to reach that galaxy and we don't have that much time. Right? We are in the making of more than a thousand spacecrafts. The one in which you all will be travelling will be closely scrutinised. So, you 5 will be the first ones to start the journey and will be in a 3-day observation. If no problem occurs then we will be sending others also one by one. The other spacecrafts have the capacity of a thousand people each. Now, are there any more questions?' I got filled with rage after listening to that plan. 'Hey, just stop, is this a joke going on? And if it is please stop it as I am in no mood to laugh. I know there is no option currently but there can be. I can find out another option, but I just need some time.' 'And time is what we don't have, Marcus' ISRO's president spoke. 'I just need three days and after three days I will be ready with an option and if I am not, I will be ready to do as you say but with that time, I also need complete access to the control room.' With this NASA's president spoke, 'Alright, I agree to give you three days, but these three days are not going to change to the fourth and you have the access to the control room.'

With this, the meeting concluded and it was made clear that the imminent three days were going to be the most critical days for the future of the planet.

Chapter Four
HELP

The next day all the group members assembled, and we began the discussion. Before I could say anything, Jay spoke 'Hey Marcus how did you get to know about all this and why didn't you tell us about all this before. Don't we have that right to know about such things which could put our lives at stake?'

'Hey, calm down miss. We just got to know about this the day before you got to know about it, and it was late in the night, so we couldn't tell you guys anything about this.' Stewart suddenly spoke up in my defense.

'Thanks, Stewart, for standing up for me. But I don't need your help, I can take care of things myself. I have been given a mouth to speak too.' Stewart looked a bit disillusioned but didn't say anything.

'As everyone assuredly heard yesterday, about how much trouble we are already in. We need to find something, and find something quickly because we don't seem to have much time. I hope that everyone agrees with me about how bad the plan thought of by our superiors is. If anyone supports it or has any concerns regarding anything they can tell me right now.' I waited a few seconds before continuing again. 'So, everyone must start working and try to look out for something good, something extraordinary, something which could help us change this decision, and if you find something, the first person you'll be reporting will be me.' After this everyone started working and I did the same too.

2 days passed and I was seeing them pass by because there was nothing in my hand that I could do instead of trying. I remember a quote I have read somewhere 'Hard work betrays none' but this time my belief in that quote was over. I started to think that death was near to us attracting us as a black hole does and no power in the universe could stop it.

I was sitting in the control room, head down and completely frustrated, with a million things going inside my mind. And I didn't know what to think about.

After a few minutes, Stewart approached me.

'Hey, boss.' He came in smiling. 'How's it going?'

'What do you think?' I replied, with a bit of exasperation in my voice.

'You seem like you have just lost. Accepted defeat without reaching the end. That's not the Marcus Robinson I know. The Marcus Robinson I know would never stop trying until the end. He would not give up without seeing everything through at least.'

'I haven't accepted defeat.' I shouted.

'But it seems you have.'

'No, I haven't. At least I didn't just lie and broke a promise I made to my best friend.' I said, regretting it immediately after I did.

'Ouch! That hurt.' He said and went away.

'No, wait! I didn't mean that.' I said, feeling bad after telling him those things.

He looked back for a second, 'Yeah, sure you did.' And went away.

MAKOTO STEWART (MONOLOGUE)

I never thought that I'd lose my best friend like this. It was all my fault.

I have always been a cheerful and extroverted guy, who loves having fun with friends, making jokes, etc. Though I have always been loved my whole life, I have had tough times too. And all of it because of my laziness. A lot of people take someone being lazy with a grain of salt but it has cost me a lot in my life. I once got extremely close to being kicked out of my university because of it too. My behaviour of cherishing rest above a lot of things has cost me a lot, which now cost me my friend. The one person I always thought will stay with me, is now gone.

Mark has always been a great friend to me, ever since all 100 of us came here from different parts of the world all alone. I was tremendously anxious with everything happening, going away from home, being given such huge responsibility, everything was messing with my head. But he made me feel at home. I never expected him to see through my emotions (I thought I was great at putting up a poker face) and approach me, talk to me, and try to calm me down. Ever since then, he became like my best bud, and in that lonely place there was still happiness and, in that hope, there was still light.

Chapter Five
A CHANCE

Today was the last day and I was hoping that we must find something today which could distract everyone's mind and get the decision changed.

Time was passing by, and I was sitting on a chair just in front of the huge screen from which I was expecting a lot. There was nothing I could do, and neither could anyone else.

'Time will pass away but we must never lose hope as even at the end that one light of hope can make your life colourful.' I read this while I was young and was surfing the net. Those lines touched deep in my heart and from then on, I had never lost hope in my life but today was something different and I was seeing my life go into complete chaos with everyone else in the whole world.

When I was a child, I was a very friendly and caring person but I didn't have any true best friends. It was just because I never showed how much I cared about them and always hid my feelings, showing myself as a self-obsessed guy. I was always sad but instead of showing I was sad I was trying to make others happy by putting a smiling face on my mouth and putting the need of other people before me but I never showed them that I was trying to do so and always hid it. I do the same now also which makes me an emotionless and self-obsessed person. I do feel bad about what they say but I never share my feelings to try to make them feel better.

At that moment, I was ready to do whatever it took to save my people even if it leads me to death but I was not ready to do something completely senseless which could lead to the death of everyone.

A few minutes later a new moon appeared on the screen which was huge and about the size of Mars. It was just as close to the earth as was earth's real moon close to the earth. It was a temporary moon.

I rushed to the head department to tell them about what I have found. I told them about the temporary moon I have found and they gave my team another day to research it to find out if it was habitable.

That was the time my hope came back and I was not hopeless. I just wanted to make this right and save the life of everyone on this planet.

Chapter Six

WORSE TIMES

After working for straight 10 hours, we found out that, the moon was a temporary one with a rocky surface and 40% chance of water availability. We prophesied that the moon will stay at its current position for about a month and then will move towards Alpha Centauri which is supposed to be 4.22 light years away. This moon had a 60% possibility of being habitable. Therefore, at least one generation of human beings could live on that moon.

With this much information, I went to the board and after about 2 hours of discussion they asked me to send some astronauts down to that moon to research it better and by the time they do so I will have to think about the future planning of humanity. About what will happen after 100 years or so. A solution to one of the biggest problems currently.

The astronauts were going to the moon for about a week and all I have to do was think about the future of the human race. This sounds easy when said but is insane when done.

The temperature was rising day by day. It started to feel hotter day by day. I didn't know what to think or what to do. I was starting to feel that something was going wrong.

I called Jay to help me find the problem. We did a bit of research and then after about an hour, we found out that the earth was coming closer to the sun. Like very close, very fast. It was as if the sun was attracting it like a magnet, and we had no idea what was happening. I spoke 'Oh, God. For fuck's sake. What the hell is happening now.'

'Calm down Mark. Everything will be fine.'

I replied sarcastically 'Yeah, sure. I can see that. Everything's gonna be fine after 1 week when we all will be burned into ashes.'

'You are wrong.'

'What?'

'We still have two weeks before that happens.' She said laughing.

'Couldn't you stop with those replies now? All of this is very serious,' I replied.

'I will, when you stop making sarcastic comments and acting like a cry-baby. Also, everything will be fine. You must keep hope. We still have 2 weeks before everything. I am sure we will find a way.'

'Yeah, in hell there are. We don't even know the reason this is happening and without it, we will never be able to find a solution. At least, not in this lifetime.'

'Mark, we will find it. Calm down, we must keep looking.'

'Oh, okay. Yeah, sure. We will find the issue of this problem. Maybe just look behind the sun. Maybe the sun is hiding it.

She looked at me surprised. Like she just found something out. 'What?' I spoke. She pushed me away and started to move the satellite through the screen behind the sun.

'What the Fuck. This is much worse than I thought.' I pushed her aside and looked at the screen. In just a fraction of a second, I was worried, sad, and hopeless again.

'Oh, man! We all are going to die.' I said, filled with fear.

'No, we will not. There must be a way out.'

'Not when there is a black hole ready to suck us in.'

'Mark, you're doing it again.' She gazed at me.

But when she saw the fear and sadness in my eyes, her expression changed.

'Oh, come on. Those pretty blue eyes don't look good when they're sad.' She said smiling, and I smiled back.

She was very positive with everything she said. It was like she was filled with hope. The hope that I was always filled with, the hope that I had lost along the way and the hope that I thought will never come back.

When I was leaving, she shouted from behind, 'Hey Mark, miracles happen, don't they!' I smiled and left.

Chapter Seven

MIRACLES DO HAPPEN

I was sitting in my room, depressed. I didn't know what to do or where to go. I had no idea. I was frustrated. I was PRAYING. For the first time in my life, I was PRAYING. I was praying to God to help me. I was praying for a miracle to happen. I knew we'd be soon dead. But there was nothing I could do instead of praying. I had no faith in God until then, I never believed that miracles could happen and until now I always had hope.

A few hours later, I got a call from Jay. I was hoping for good news. But the news I got could not be put in a single category. The news I got was neither good nor bad. Jay said that they have found a sudden conception of another black hole. She said that it appeared out of nowhere.

With this, it was confirmed that a collision was going to happen between the black holes. Now the main question was what was going to happen after the collision. I had a few theories about that. But what I wished to be true was the creation of a worm hole.

I went to Jay and asked her about the size of the hole and was it bigger than the black hole. She told me what I hoped for. Their sizes were exactly the same. This significantly increased the chances of a wormhole creation. I was happy after a long time and my hope came back. This time I wasn't going to let it go.

Filled with happiness and hope, I started rushing to go to the board to tell them about it, suddenly Jay shouted 'Hey Mark, told you so.'

I said to myself 'Mark, your prayers have been heard. And yes, Jay you were right, miracles do happen.'

Chapter Eight
THE DECISIVE DAY

I clarified everything to the board. After I explained them, I started getting mixed reactions. After about 5 minutes a member of the board spoke to me 'How can this happen?' and before I could say anything the head of the department spoke 'They did it.' I found myself a bit confused. I didn't know who they were but I wanted to. The whole place went into a mood of silence, but after a few minutes of it I finally asked him 'Who are they?' 'Nobody knows who are they. But if they have done this, it means that they want us to live.' After saying this he dismissed me and told me that they will discuss this and will let me and my team know about what they have thought to do.

I collected my team and explained to them the circumstances. I again started seeing mixed reactions. Some were terrified while others were neutral.

When I saw those reactions, I spoke 'This is good news everyone.'

Before I could say anything else, Vishnu cut me 'How the hell in god's name is this good news. We are standing on the brink of death and you are saying that this is good news.'

Suddenly Jay spoke in my defense 'Hey, this is good news because we are standing on the brink of death and through this, we can get a chance to live. These days we have been through worse than this. So now we have got a chance to live and we must take it and try to live.'

James (The head of the board) called me into his office to discuss the mission.

'Hello Marcus, so as you can see, we are currently going through really tough times where we don't even know if we will be able to live or we will die. Now I am going to ask you some questions concerning the collision and I want straight facts. Okay?'

'Yes, sir.'

'So, what is the percentage of a worm hole creation with the collision?'

'Sir, 60%.'

'If the worm hole gets created what are the chances, we could travel through it?'

'Sir, as you know if the worm hole gets created it will be very close to the sun…'

Before I could say anything else, he shouted 'Marcus, tell me straight answers.'

'Sir, 30%'

'Ok, now you can go.'

While I was leaving, I turned my face towards James and said 'Sir, but there is also a chance that, while the collision is happening the sun could go inside the black hole. Which will increase our chances of going inside the worm hole and going through it.' After saying this I left.

The very next day, about 50 huge spacecrafts were made ready for travel.

I was seeing them getting prepared while James approached me and put his hand on my back 'According to my calculations, the collision is going to happen tomorrow and we don't want to risk our chances so we will be taking off today. These 50 spacecrafts will be enough to load every human being on this planet.'

He patted me on the back 'Come on boy, get ready for the launch,' and then he smiled at me.

I was really happy that he listened to me. I was very happy and I couldn't explain how happy I was. It felt like this was going to be right.

There was a meeting of all the crew and we were told that we will be starting taking off in 4 hours. Each spacecraft will be going towards Jupiter for precaution if any explosion happens. After the collision happens the main spacecraft will lead the way and the others will follow.

The main spacecraft was the biggest one and it consisted of space for about 5 million people. The main crew, our families, our friends and their families, our relatives everyone was allowed to board that spacecraft. My team and I were going to be in that spacecraft as well.

Chapter Nine
THE UNEXPECTABLE

It was launch time for our spacecraft. Everyone had boarded the craft, not even a single one was left. The launches were scheduled in two minutes gap. Which meant that it would take 100 minutes for each aircraft to launch.

We were leaving earth. We were leaving our home planet. We were leaving the planet where we have lived for billions of years. I was standing on the land just beside the spacecraft for the last time. I just wanted to say a proper goodbye to my home planet. I don't usually cry; I never cry, but this time I cried. I started sobbing. I cried until I heard the call 'We are ready to launch.'

We were ready to launch and I was the pilot. The countdown began and with the countdown, our last moments on earth began. I was seeing my home plant for the last time.

We took off successfully and in no time, we reached near Jupiter. After the successful take-off, the board members came to congratulate me and my team. I didn't want to hear congratulations not because the mission wasn't complete but because all I was thinking about was earth.

It took approximately 2 hours for each spacecraft to reach its allotted position. We were to spend the night in the spacecrafts only. Rooms were allotted to each person. Their size depended upon a person's position, or some people were given huge rooms when they paid for them.

I was trying to sleep all night, but I wasn't able to sleep. I just kept thinking about what will happen the next day. The next day, I went to the bathroom to freshen myself up. When I turned on the shower to take a bath, I saw something insanely crazy. Instead of water, blood was coming out of the shower. I got terrified and ran out of my room. I saw that nobody besides me had woken up. Then, suddenly all the lights turned on. I could see different kinds of images on my screen.

I was terrified. I didn't know what to do so I ran into Jay's room and woke her up.

I started to stutter 'Blood…lights…screen.'

She hugged me tightly, 'Calm down Mark.'

She then made me sit on a chair and gave me a glass of water. 'Now tell me, what happened?'

I spoke hastily, 'Come with me. Fast.'

I held her hand and took her where the screen was blinking. She saw that but she didn't look horrified, and she took everything very calmly. She took out her tab and tech pen. She then started writing something.

'These are not normal pictures. This is Morse code. Look.'

When I looked at her tab I was astounded and muddled 'Save them?'

'Yeah, do you know what it means?'

'No, I have absolutely no idea. I think we must show this to James.'

'No, we must figure out what is the problem ourselves and then show it to him. I think he will not do anything.'

'Yes, you are right. But we must try to figure out the problem before it's too late.'

It was the time of the collision, and I was still tensed and afraid thinking about what'd just happened to me and what did the message mean.

The collision wasn't as was expected, it wasn't a good one and it wasn't a bad one. The result wasn't from one of the possibilities, it was completely unbelievable.

When the collision was happening, I wasn't looking at it, I was looking at the hopeful eyes of the people. That was giving me strength. It was giving me the power to stand strong and look forward. But, before I could even turn my head towards the screen, I lost my sight. I could see black light, wherever I saw for about 2 minutes. Then suddenly there was a blackout, and I fainted.

I thought, 'This wasn't supposed to happen, how could any of this happen! What the hell! Someone must do something.' And suddenly I woke up.

Chapter Ten

WHAT HAPPENED?

~~~ ~~~ ~~~

When I woke up, I saw that I wasn't the only one who fainted, everyone else fainted too.

Before I could do anything, Delano shouted 'Mark!' He was standing a few feet away, behind me. 'Come on, fast… I think there is something wrong.' I followed him to the control room. When we reached there, I saw that we were no other spacecrafts besides ours, like they disappeared into thin air.

But this wasn't the main problem. They were not the ones who disappeared into thin air, we were the ones who did. We were not in a milky way anymore. I didn't know where we were. It was like we travelled through space without going inside the wormhole. This also meant that other spacecrafts must've travelled too. This meant that every other spacecraft was also roaming in the universe not knowing where they are.

The biggest surprise was that we were in a galaxy unknown to mankind. I was surprised to see this. According to me, we have covered each galaxy within 20 billion light years from our planet. This was very irritating.

I then went to Jay. When I reached there, she was reading an e-book.

'Hey, Mark.' As always, she sounded very calm. But this was not the time to be calm. I was filled with emotions.
~~~

'I found out what the message meant.'

'Oh, congratulations Mark! I figured it out at the time of the collision.'

I spoke furiously 'Then, why the hell didn't you tell me?'

'You know why.'

'No, I don't.' My anger was turning into a rage, and I wasn't able to calm myself down after I saw Jay so tension-free.

'Because there was no time. Before I could tell anyone, the explosion happened.'

'So, now we have simply just failed the mission. We weren't able to crack the code down before the collision and now we have lost what we could have saved.'

I then calmed myself down 'Oh okay, now we must go and explain the current situation to James.'

'Yeah, let's go.'

We went to James and told him about the situation.

'What should we do next sir?'

'There's nothing we could do. Go and focus on the future. We must save the others. Try and find habitable planets for the future of mankind.'

The way he spoke sounded suspicious. It sounded like he knew what was going to happen.

After a few minutes of standing there, I finally asked him 'Did you know that this was going to happen?'

'Go to your room Mark, and get some rest,' he replied.

I raised my voice and asked again 'Did. You. Know. What was. Going to. Happen!'

'Yes, I knew what was going to happen. Now…'

Before he could say anything else, I held him by the collar angrily 'Why didn't you tell us about it? Why didn't you try to save them?'

'Because I couldn't Mark. I couldn't. It was better for 5 million people to be safe than the death of everyone trying to stick together.'

I left his collar and he dropped on the floor 'Yes you could, but you didn't.'

Then I stormed out of the room. Jay was standing outside, she tried to stop me, but I didn't and I went to my room without taking a single stop filled with rage, frustration, and tension thinking about what had happened to the others.

Chapter Eleven
WHAT SHOULD I DO NOW

Like always, I didn't sleep that night. I felt that seeing these difficult times pass by was very frustrating. When James told me about the huge game he had played, I got angry. I was filled with rage. It was like I would have killed him if I got the chance. But as you know, nothing's ever that easy.

I didn't go to work the next day. I sat in my room, on the floor beside my bed, with a bottle of alcohol in my hand. I drank all day.

I didn't even know what I did while I was drunk. The very next day, I woke up and found Jay sitting on the chair in front of me, her hazel eyes glaring at me and her lips giving me a soft smile. She felt like she hadn't slept all day. I, then looked around and saw that it was not my room 'Where am I?'

She stood up and sat next to me 'You're in my room, genius.'

'What the hell happened?'

'You better not ask that,' she said laughingly.

'Why?'

'Oh my god, I can't even start to explain the wonders you did yesterday.'

'Did you sleep? You look like you haven't slept all day.'

'Oh, that's because I was indulged in trying to save you from doing something horrible'

I stood up rubbing my eyes with my hands 'So, did I puke?'

'Yeah, about 2 times. The first time you destroyed my dress, but I saved another dress the second time. But that wasn't enough for you so, you destroyed my heels the second time you puked.'

'Oh my god! I am sorry. You must've had a crappy day.'

'No, you can't say that. I don't know if you realise it or not, but you are a really funny man.'

'Yeah, I save that for when I get drunk.'

'So, why did you drink that much alcohol. I mean it was too much alcohol for an addict too.'

I smiled a little 'Yeah, I think so. It was maybe because I have been having a bunch of shitty days or you can say the worst days of my life.'

'Why?' She held my hands into hers tightly 'Come on, tell me about it.'

'No, it's nothing.'

'Come on…. Tell me. I know it's something.'

'I am telling you. You really wouldn't want to hear my depressing story.'

'Hey… Why don't you want to tell me?'

'No, it's not that I don't want to tell you. It's just that no one has ever asked me about myself. I've had a lot of friends, and a lot of people in my life but until now, nobody has asked me about my feelings or how am I doing, or anything related to me. I've always seen myself trying to make them happy, helping them solve their problems, and trying to keep them safe.'

Then before I could say anything else, she hugged me. She hugged me tightly, it was a bit uncomfortable, but I didn't care and hugged her back. This was the first time someone had cared for me and made me feel like there was someone for me.

While she was hugging me, she said 'Take no more tension. Calm down and now think about the future because you can't change the past. We need to save them.'

'Thank you, Jay. I owe you one,' I said to her, and she smiled.

MARCUS ROBINSON (MONOLOGUE)

I had grown up in a very happy and happening environment since my childhood with both of my parents always there for me. I didn't face a lot of problems when I was a kid. I'd say that I had a pretty normal life until 3032 came.

I am a very simple-minded person, seeing situations in black and white, fighting for what I believe in, being extremely stubborn for the things I want, and speaking the ugly truths no one ever wants to hear. Though I have always wanted to find people I could be close to, someone who tells me all their secrets and someone who I could share my secrets with. Someone who stands up for me when I need them to and someone who lets me fight for them. Someone who loves me for who I am and for what I am. This is the only thing anyone ever wants, and that is what I have been trying to find my whole life. Trying to find someone who can just be like a family to me.

I have never experienced any real struggle throughout my life like others might have. My mom and dad had always tried to provide me with the best lifestyle possible, no matter what, and I am very thankful for that. Everything had been perfect in my life. But then, about 5 years ago my dad had died. I was not a kid then, so I probably was able to handle it better and help my mom with coping with the loss too both emotionally and financially. It was a hard time for both of us, I was completely broken. Thinking about it now too becomes very difficult for me.

Thankfully my mom was still alive, there to support me and help me with my decisions. I always used to call her whenever I was free from my duties, talk about my day, and ask about hers. She always used to talk to me so cheerfully, but I knew that she was just trying to hide the hole left inside her heart by putting on a mask. Sometimes I used to go visit her too whenever there was nothing to do in the spacecraft.

Chapter Twelve
THE EARTH

All these spacecrafts were made for the first mission. But that one got cancelled because of me, so a lot of them were combined to decrease the number of spacecrafts and make the capacity inside them bigger. All the hibernation pods were also removed to create more space. So out of 1000 huge spacecrafts, 50 gigantic spacecrafts were made, and you could imagine what that would look like.

We had our private robots on earth. They were like our friends. They did whatever we said them to do and talked to us whenever we wanted. I named mine 'Emily'. I was really missing her. But, like everything they were not allowed to take with us to create more space as they were like a normal human being, and they couldn't afford robots travelling with us.

I loved the earth. We left a lot of cool things like this on earth. Also, a few old people were not allowed to board the spacecrafts because they were dying. I felt bad for them but like always there was nothing I could do.

The one thing they had in large amounts on the spacecraft was alcohol. I mean 'WTF', you could leave old people to die for your addiction. It was like they were murderers. They could murder people to drink a bottle of alcohol.

It was a lot different in the spacecraft. A lot of things changed from earth to spacecraft. But the one thing that didn't change was the fucked-up people.

***

Ever Since we left earth, I had made a habit of roaming around the spacecraft while everyone was asleep. Going around and checked up on our home, which the spacecraft had become. Usually, I used to run into passengers who would often greet me. A lot would even ask me questions about stuff regarding our plans, etc. Some of them were quite anxious too, I tried to calm them down, give them a light of hope, and give them the much-needed assurance. But in reality, I was terrified.

The spacecraft was designed with a lot of thought being put into making it feel more home-like, more earth-like. A lot of facilities like an artificial jungle, an artificial river, and even different bedroom styles were put in. Stuff for entertainment purposes like movie theatres, amusement and water parks, malls, spas, etc. Everything you had on earth was given to you to make it feel more like you never left. But never a moment passed by that I didn't miss the earth.

Chapter Thirteen

THE RESEARCH BEGINS

The next day I started working again, started working hard like I always do. I had nothing else in my mind except 'how to remain alive?'

It took about 6 hours to get all the information about the star and its surrounding planets. The first problem came in when I found out that the star was 1000% hotter than our sun. Which meant that its lifeline was about 40 million years. But that wasn't the problem. The problem was that the planets were hot. All the planets were hot. Leaving one, which was the last planet in the series. It was the farthest from the sun. But the problem was that it was cold and hot. It means that half of the planet was cold, and half was hot. The cold part had a temperature of about -100 degrees Celsius while the hot part had a temperature of about 100 degrees Celsius. No human has ever lived in that kind of temperature.

Which meant that we had a total loss. We had nowhere to go. We all were probably going to die. But I didn't want to let that happen. This time I wasn't going to lose hope. This time I was going to fight for our lives.

I was working hard to find a solution. It was about 2 in the morning when Stewart came into the control room. He was wearing his night suit. It looked like he couldn't sleep.

'Hey Mark, what are you doing up?'

'I could ask you the same question.'

'Yeah, I wasn't able to sleep so I decided to take a walk. What about you?'

'I am working. I need to find something before it's too late. I need to find a solution. I must...'

'Stop... Stop man. You must rest. If you keep doing this, you'll die before anything else. Go and sleep. We'll talk about this with James.'

I replied in anger 'there's no fuckin' way that I'm going to talk to that son of a bitch 'bout anything. Don't you know the game he'd played!'

'I know what he's done. But do you have a better option? He's far more experienced than us and is the best shot we have got.' He took a brief pause and then spoke 'Also, I am sorry for all that I said and did. I know I was at fault; I should have done something about it. I am sorry.' He said while looking down.

'Hey, I am sorry too. It was my fault too. I always knew you were a lazy ass.' I said laughing. 'But really, I didn't give you enough time to be able to do anything and then I acted harshly towards you after that. I am so sorry.'

With that we became friends again, I guess we both realised our mistakes, and I was very happy to get my bestie back too.

After that, I went into my room and tried to take a nap.

Chapter Fourteen
WHAT IS HAPPENING?

I slept for hardly 2 hours the other day. When I stepped outside my room, I witnessed something surprising and confusing. There was a rush everywhere. The whole area was crowded with people. I went straight into the control room, and I saw my whole team there without me.

'What the Fuck's happening and why wasn't I informed?' I asked.

Delano replied, 'We didn't want to disturb you, Mark.'

Vishnu grinned 'Hey, we've got good news. We are back on our home planet. I mean, we will be back on our home planet. But we have reached the solar system.'

'How?'

'I don't know how. No one knows how. Maybe it's just another miracle.'

'But it must have been destroyed by now.'

'Yeah, we know that. But it hasn't. Instead, it is like it was years ago. We are just doing some research before we land on earth.'

'No, stop it. No one will do anything without my instructions,' I ordered them and left.

I was very confused. Something surely didn't feel right about what'd happened. I went to James to tell him about this. When I entered his room, he was wandering all around the place. It was like he was thinking about something.

Before I could say anything, he started speaking 'I know what's happening.'

'So, isn't that good? Why aren't you excited? We are back in our solar system.'

'This isn't our solar system, Mark.'

'Then which solar system is this?'

'The question isn't 'which solar system is this?' the question you should be asking is 'Which universe is this?''

I was confused about what I heard from James. When he saw my lost expression, he said 'Yes Mark, you heard it right. Don't seem so lost. We are not in our universe. And my best guess is that we are in our parallel universe.'

'But how could this happen?'

'How could any of this happen, Mark? How could two blackholes appear out of nowhere! How could we be magically transported into a galaxy we have no idea about! Mark, everything here doesn't have a proper explanation. Everything here is weird. Everything's happening is insane and we can't explain any of it. But what you can do is to try your best to understand. Try your best to understand that everything which is happening, is happening for the best. You must be grateful that we all are alive. Not these 5 million people but every person who boarded the spacecraft that day is alive. I know that all of us aren't together now, but all of us are alive and you must be grateful for that. I know you'll do right by us Mark. You just need to put faith in yourself.'

'How do you know that? You don't even know me.'

'I know you enough Mark. You are much more capable than you think you are. You are very special and are bound to do great things.'

Chapter Fifteen

A SURPRISING ENCOUNTER

I was roaming around the spacecraft at night like I usually did when I found Jay walking around too. She looked a bit pale than before. She used to be very happy usually, roaming around making jokes, being overly sarcastic, more like putting on a mask because I'd never seen her sad. So really, I was seeing a side of her that she hid from everyone.

I decided to go and check up on her.

'Hey, what's got you all down?' I asked while moving towards her.

'Nothing. Just thinking about stuff.'

When I got close to her, I pulled her towards me by her hand and hugged her. No matter how sad you get or no matter how many faces you put on. Sometimes all you need is a hug to calm you and help heal that feeling. The moment I saw her, I knew it wasn't 'nothing'. No matter how much she tried to hide it.

I hugged her, and a few seconds later I saw a tear drop down her eyes but she immediately hid it by rubbing it off her face. At that moment, my suspicions were confirmed. That she wasn't fine, not then, not before.

'You know you don't have to hide 'yourself' with me,' I said, still hugging her.

'Hmmm,' she replied.

Chapter Sixteen

WHO ARE THEY?

James' words had a huge impact on me. According to me, those words were to make me motivated. But it didn't happen. Instead, I felt pressurised. I never thought that people expected so much from me. This was all new to me and I didn't know what to do with it.

I also got to see a new part of Jay, and some part of me wanted to help her as she helped me.

After laying down on my bed for some time I got up to go to the control room. But before I could go anywhere something strange and dangerous happened. Something hit the spacecraft. It destroyed almost 1/4th of the spacecraft. Then when I reached the control room; I saw the worried and afraid faces of my team. And suddenly an astral projection of a person appeared right in front of us. 'Stay away from us. Return the hell to where you came from,' he said.

I rushed to the system in the control room 'Show me how much damage is done?' I spoke. The results the monitor showed were bad. 25% of the spacecraft was demolished. This was going to be bad for us.

Before anything else, complaints started coming. Each person was complaining. A lot of machines were not working properly, and a lot of machines were not working entirely. This was not the biggest priority. The biggest priority was to ensure that we stay alive. But after what'd happened, I was afraid that this was going to be the end for us.

Chapter Seventeen
DON'T GO

This incident made one thing very clear these people were far more advanced than us and were going to kill us if we didn't disappear from their solar system.

Before I could try to take care of the damages, I would have to ensure that no more damage was to be done. For this to happen, we were to disappear before the next attack. In such conditions, it was difficult for the spacecraft to move.

I was in the control room with my team trying to find a solution to the problem. 'Vishnu; which parts of the system are damaged?' I asked.

'All the main machinery seem alright to me. The customer services have malfunctioned. But there is something we are missing. Something else has malfunctioned too and that is the reason the spacecraft isn't working properly and is not moving.'

'Oh okay, keep working and I'll be right back,' I said and left.

I was very worried. I wasn't sure what'd happened and what was going to happen. Everything was a mystery. Both time and space were playing with us. They were playing a game we can never win. I wanted everyone to be alive. If I were asked to give my life for them to live, I would give it in a second. But that wasn't the case. If anyone died and I lived, I would blame myself for their death

While I was walking, I saw Jay running towards me 'Mark… stop,' She shouted. I stopped and waited for her. She was wearing her spacesuit. When she came, she said 'I found the reason the spacecraft's not working properly.'

I smiled 'What is it?'

'It's the jet. The jet on the left side of the back of the spacecraft is having a problem. One of its doors is closed.'

'Then why did you come here? You should have gone to the control room to that.'

'I already tried it. It isn't working.'

'Then we'll find another way,' I said. 'Also, why are you wearing your spacesuit.'

'Mark, we have to do it manually. That's why I have worn the spacesuit.'

'No, there must be another way to do that.'

'No Mark, there is no other way.'

I shouted in fear 'you could die. Don't you understand that?'

She put her hand on my shoulder 'I know Mark.'

'You don't know anything. When you manually open the door, a lot of heat will come rushing in and you could die. I won't allow you to do that.'

'No Mark, I have to do it. I have done a lot of terrible things in my life, things you wouldn't believe that I could do, and this is the only way to my redemption. I must and I will do it. You have to let me go.'

After saying this she ran. I tried to stop her. But before I could do anything else, she was gone.

I got sad; it was like tears were forcing me to let them come out. But before anything, I went straight to the control room. 'Where is Jay?' I asked. Stewart pointed at the screen; she was alive. I got a bit relieved seeing her alive. But she was going into the mouth of death itself. I took the microphone in hurry and put it in front of my mouth. 'Jay? Do you hear me? I order you to stop. I won't allow you to do this.' 'Sorry Mark, but I can't do what you're saying.' She said and then turned off the communication.

'Don't do this. Jay stop… please stop,' I cried. In a few minutes, she opened the door and heat came rushing. I saw her. I saw her helmet breaking. I couldn't do anything. She was dying right in front of me. Her helmet completely broke and she glared at me the last time with a smile on her face. Even at the time of her death, she was smiling. She was smiling like everything was alright and like nothing had happened. She died happily but left me all alone.

I was completely broken up. I sobbed and sobbed. 'How could you do this to me? Why did you do this…' I kept saying. Stewart came to me and hugged me. 'Everything will be alright Mark. She did her job, and we must honour her for the sacrifice she made,' he said.

Chapter Eighteen
I MISS YOU

You left. You didn't even think about what'd happen to those who cared about you. You didn't think about what would happen to me.

I was missing your glare. I was missing your beautiful eyes. I was missing your smile. I was missing your calm and cool attitude. That attitude annoyed me a lot. I was missing it. I wanted you to irritate me, annoy me, make me angry. Do anything you wanted to do. I promise I will smile no matter what you do. Just come back, I miss you.

About 4 days passed, after her death. We'd started moving away from that earth before anything bad happened. Every second, every minute, and every hour I saw passing by, I missed her more. All I could do was think about her.

It was about 10:00 pm, I was laying down on my bed and something surprising happened. A Flyctor (It is like a fly. It is a projector. Used to send 3D video messages.) came from the bottom of my bed. It was a message from Jay.

'Hey, Mark. I know you must be sad after my death. And if you're not, you are an ass. Now I am going to say what I made this video to say whether you want to listen or not. Okay, so… by the time you get it I will be dead. But if I am not close to this and you mustn't see it otherwise, I will never talk to you. I laughed a bit. 'But if I am… I just want to say that I am thankful to God to have given me such a sweet and nice and kind and handsome and somewhat cool friend like you… Oh F***! Did I just praise you too much? Don't you laugh Mr. Robinson.' I grinned a bit. 'You are a great man, Mark. I know you'll miss me, but I'd be really happy if you would not miss me that much. You have a great life ahead of you Mark. I have accomplished my destiny. But yours is much bigger than me, it is bigger than all of us. You are the only one who could save them. You must try your best. And you owe me one, remember…' 'How could I forget,' I said smiling. 'So, I want you to be happy, miss me less but miss me or I will haunt you in your dreams,' she said laughing. 'Have faith in yourself Mark, put confidence in yourself, and don't stop, keep moving forward. Also, I want you to fall in love with an attractive and wonderful girl and when this is all over, buy yourself a very nice home, an amazing car, and have an epic life and family with a beautiful wife and kids. I am proud of you Mark.'

I smiled 'This was a good closure,' I said to myself. I didn't cry, instead, I smiled. I thought about her and smiled.

Chapter Nineteen

ON THE MOVE

We were moving far away from that earth, far away from that solar system, and far away from those arrogant people.

We were uninterruptedly on the move because we didn't know where we were and where we'd to go.

'Hey Mark, we must tell James and the board about this situation and ask them about what step to be taken next,' Delano said.

'No, Delano. No one is going to go to James or the board. We, right here, are the only ones who make the important decisions. They may have been leaders on earth, but now, they aren't. And this must remain the same way,' I replied.

While we were arguing about whether to tell the board or not, the spacecraft started moving faster. A lot faster. It felt like we were moving at the speed of light. 'Speed over limit' was shown in the system. I didn't what to do so I just stood still. I looked around and everything was still. It was like time had stopped. Then, a few moments later the spacecraft stopped. I rushed to the system to look where we were. Thanks to God, we were back into our solar system. And for once it was it was detected by our operating system.

I tried to look around and I saw that all the planets were the same but something else was deeply upsetting. The sun looked kind of old. It was like it had come to its end. Then, I saw that it had a black hole just beside it.

'Okay; so now this whole thing is creeping me out,' Delano said.

'We are in our solar system. But we are not in the time we should be in. We are way into the future. Now we have a black hole and an upcoming black hole in front of us. What the fuck do we do now?' Vishnu said.

I looked at him and said 'Hey man, calm down. We'll think of something.'

'When will we think of something. When we all will die? Huh?' he spoke in rage.

'Do you have any better idea?' I asked.

'No, but I know one thing for sure that if even one thing goes wrong, we all could die. So, for the sake of God, do something, Mark.'

Before I could say anything, Delano spoke 'Let's go into the black hole?'

'What the fuck are you talking about?' Vishnu said. 'Are you literally out of your mind?'

I remained quiet while Vishnu was blabbing at him for completely no reason. I was considering Delano's idea of going inside the black hole. After 5 minutes I put a stop to the argument and spoke 'Yeah, let's do it. Let's go into the black hole. Delano's right. If the theories are correct, they can help us travel into space and time, and that's what we need. Right guys?'

Vishnu was not impressed with what I said, and he again started speaking bullshit. 'No, there's no way in hell we are going to do that. Do you know what could…'?

'Yeah, let's do it,' Stewart shouted.

Vishnu tried to stop us, but we didn't and went straight for it.

Before going into the black hole Stewart asked, 'Are you ready?' 'Yes,' I replied. 'So, let's go,' he said, and then we went into it taking hopes of billions of people with us.

Chapter Twenty

WHOSE FAULT WAS IT?

I was filled with different kinds of emotions at that time. I didn't know what to think or speak or even feel. I felt nothing but everything. This decision was going to decide our lives and I was just hoping to get a positive reaction.

When we entered the black hole, everything went dark. We couldn't see a thing. What we saw was darkness. Everyone panicked.

After a few minutes, I started feeling like everything was disappearing. Earlier, everyone was talking, but now I didn't hear a voice. I was not able to feel the ground beneath me. Like there was no spacecraft and I was all alone in a place of nowhere.

I shouted 'Hello; anyone here?... Stewart... Delano...' I heard nothing. I couldn't hear my voice. I got scared. I felt it was going to be the end of my life. I was afraid that I was going to die there and disappear into the universe.

After some time, I found myself back in the spacecraft and my friends standing all around. They were talking and laughing. 'Hey Mark, look we are back,' Stewart said(laughing).

Everything was becoming weirder by the second. I looked around, and I saw our solar system. I got a bit relieved and happy. But then, we saw that a black hole was created beside our sun.

We did some research and found out that we were in our past. We were at the time when the temporary moon appeared.

This meant that it was our fault. The black holes were created because of us. All of this was our fault and now there was nothing we could do.

We made a different decision in the past, which led to this future, leading to the creation of this black hole.

After some hours of frustration and disappointment, I went to James to tell him about the news. I told him about everything that'd happened.

He didn't seem surprised. After a few seconds of silence, he spoke, 'No Mark, it's not our fault.'

'How could you say that?' I asked.

'Come on Mark.' He said picking up a glass of wine from his table. 'You're smarter than this. Think, mark. Think.'

This talk was getting a lot more confusing than I anticipated. 'I don't understand what you're talking about.'

'Okay, so how would explain us being here? How would you explain going here and nowhere else? Why this place only? And how would you explain the speed of light, Mark?'

'Then who did it?' I asked.

'They did it, Mark. They did it.'

He was becoming more and more suspicious. He was speaking in a way that made me think that he knew a lot more than we thought he knew.

'Who are you really?' I finally asked.

'Now that's a smart question, Mark,' he said and smiled.

Now that scared me. I was terrified. I was terrified of our boss. I didn't even know if he was our boss.

What if he is not like us? What if he is from a different planet? What if he is dangerous and a threat to us?' Thoughts like these crowded my mind. I was afraid to say anything, but I couldn't leave without knowing everything.

'What the f*** are you?' I asked.

'Mark, I am not some horrible person you think I am. I am not someone from another world or a parallel universe or any possibility you could think of, Mark. I am neither devil nor God. I am neither light nor darkness. I am the one outside the realms of possibilities. I am living in its purest form. Mark, I am life itself.'

I didn't have any words to speak or to think after that. I just remained quiet and he spoke again.

'Mark, I have been pushing you, I have made sure to you were to remain alive and you are till now. I have done everything I can, and now it's your chance.' James said. 'Mark, do you want to know why you are so special?'

I didn't say a word, but I did want to know.

After a few seconds, he continued, 'You know how there is an infinite number of universes with an immeasurable number of possibilities of yourselves. In all of your infinite selves, you are dead, except this one. Even in the possibility that everyone is immortal, you are dead there also. And in all of those universes you weren't able to live past one year of age, Mark. This is the only reality where you are alive. This is what makes you special.'

After he said that, his body started turning into particles, into little particles of light. It was like he was mixing into the universe. He was turning into light. But I didn't want him to leave. I wanted to know more, I wanted to know what I should do and what was happening.

He was suddenly gone. But I still wanted to know more. I wanted to know more about him, I wanted to know more about me. I shouted at the top of my voice, hoping that an answer would come.

'What am I supposed to do with this James. Who am I really?'

And suddenly I heard a voice, 'You are the one who will save or form the end, of existence.' The voice said and then it was all quiet.

Leaving a big box of questions in my brain, he left. I wanted to know so much more. I wanted to know who he was, how did he know all this, and lastly why me?

PART 2

Reality is Non-Existent

(Jay Evans)

My Story (Jay Evans)

My life has always been a shit show. Divorced parents, a drug addict dad, and a mom who always found a new husband every few months. The longest marriage she had was probably with dad, which lasted for a few years, otherwise, no other marriage did last more than that.

I worked hard to get out of that hell hole. It just made me more depressed. I was always moving houses with my mom, never having any place to call home. I worked my ass off to get into one of the best universities in the world and worked hard there to get into one of the best organizations in the world. Out of every misery my mother ever caused me, there was one thing which she did right. It was marrying rich people. Thanks to her gorgeous looks, everyone she ever married was surprisingly rich. Except for dad, of course. That helped me in studying better too. Both my mom and dad were extremely good-looking.

My dad was also one of the few people not allowed to board the spacecraft, because of being a drug addict. I didn't care much, because he was never there for me, so why should I give a fuck. My mom also died a few years ago.

I was set on devoting my whole life to work. Doing something which would make people remember me for decades to come. Making a name for myself. Being respected. While working, I even made a few friends, which I had never imagined I would. Isabella, Rahul, Jen, and me. We all worked in the same agency.

Isabella and I were scientists, whereas Rahul and Jen were engineers. Though everyone's field of study was different.

We always gathered, had fun, went to parties, ate lunch together, did a lot of fun stuff, and enjoyed ourselves to the fullest. For the first time in my life, I was very happy. But then it happened.

Came the year 3032, and the end of my happy life started. Every top government or private organisations such as NASA, ISRO, EESA, Harvard, etc. was asked to send their best and that is when I betrayed the people, I loved the most.

I knew that I wasn't going to be selected or rather I was friends with the ones who were at the top of the list of being selected. I know I should've been happy for them but an opportunity like that had always been my dream. I just didn't wanna let it go. And I was pretty sure that if my friends weren't in the race, I'd have a high chance of success.

Rahul wasn't interested in being selected or rather, he didn't wanna add more burden to his blissful life. So, I got him to back out from it. He went to the director and asked him to remove his name from consideration. It was nice of him to do so for me. But the next was probably the worst decision I had ever made in my entire life which now looking back I regret the most.

Isabella and Jen wanted to be selected and were working their asses off for the same. But I wanted it more than them, I needed it more than them. It was my lifelong dream. I just had to be selected no matter what and the best way for me to do so was to use the truth.

In our entire time working for EESA, there was this one incident that happened but no one got to know about it. It happened while Jen and I were working on a project together. It was late night and we were almost done with it. I decided to head off early as Jen told me that she would complete the rest of the work. It was a very important project for the whole of Europe as we were gonna become the first ones to achieve a feat like that. The project was marked as the top priority and millions of euros were spent on it.

But the very next day, I found out that our machine has malfunctioned and we needed to do some changes to rectify it. But then Jen told me the truth. She was working on the project while Isabella came and they both got drunk and had fun which destroyed millions of euros worth of equipment, which they labelled as a malfunction. She also told me that they don't exactly remember what happened at that time. Then about a week later, NASA came up with the same project. And instead of us being the first ones, they were. So not only did Jen and Isabella destroy the equipment, but they also leaked the project information to NASA.

This was a huge debacle, and I told all of it to the director, hoping they get removed from consideration and I will be selected. But something far worse happened.

They both were fired from their jobs. I didn't expect that to happen. I only thought that they would just not be given preference for the selection. They didn't know who did it and they, never for a second, thought it could be me because they trusted me wholly.

But it hit Isabella harder than anyone thought. A few days later, I heard that Isabella had committed suicide by taking the death pill. It was a pill to die a comfortable death without any pain or struggle normally used to carry out death sentences or for terminal patients who wished to pull the plug. It was illegal to be used like this, but if someone tried hard, they could get their hands on one.

I never thought this could happen. She worked all her life to reach there and I took it away from her. No, not only that, I took her life away from her. Her family was poor, and she was the only support they had. She wouldn't even have gotten a job anywhere else cause of how her reputation had crashed due to the firing. I never for a moment stopped to think about her.

I didn't deserve this; I didn't deserve to live for what I'd done. My heart had completely turned black. I don't think I'd ever be able to heal from this. It will always be my fault that she was dead. It will just keep eating me inside, that guilt, until it burns me whole.

Chapter Twenty One
ALL THAT I EVER WANTED

I slowly opened my eyes; my vision was not clear; Everything seemed dark. After blinking for a bit, everything started slowly becoming clearer. And suddenly, someone hugged me and started crying.

'Oh, you're alive. I have been so worried about you Jay.' The person said crying.

The moment I heard that voice I knew. I knew it was Mark. I was so happy that he was the first one to hug me and see me. I don't know why, but I was filled with happiness, and before I knew tears were coming out of my eyes. I wanted to escape reality and live in that moment forever. Although I knew it had to end. Just before I could say anything, Mark shouted, 'She's awake.' And everyone came rushing into the room. Some were crying while some were hugging me. They were all like those people who I have only seen or met a few times, still, they were so happy that I did not die. I just couldn't believe it. Although I didn't mind, because they were happy for me.

Everything seemed perfect. It was as if, all the troubles we had, were vanished away. Then suddenly, Mark took my hand and led me away towards his room, away from all the crowd.

There he held me tight, and then kissed me. It was magical. I was left speechless. Marcus Robinson kissed me. It was great, and I was left feeling joy even after the kiss. Just when I was feeling happy, I remembered the Flyctor. I pushed him away a bit and started staring at him, putting on a brave front.

'Did u see it?' I asked

'See what?'

'The thing?'

'What thing?' He looked confused.

I then thought, 'maybe he didn't see it'

'Never mind,' I said and then pulled him close again and kissed him.

Chapter Twenty Two
DREAMING?

It was like the perfect life. Everything felt too good to be true. It felt like a dream, my dream.

Later, after our oh-so-romantic reunion, Mark told me about how everything was back to normal and earth had aged back 1000 years. I couldn't believe what I was hearing, there were doubts all over my head, but even more so it felt like a perfect world. Mark was acting like a Prince, everything was normal, and people were laughing and enjoying their lives with relief. At that moment, I really could imagine a future for me, a future for me and Mark, us together, enjoying our lives. The distant nearly impossible dream I had, was close to being true. I just wished nothing would change.

My heart wanted to believe everything I was seeing but my mind was not. It was as if, they were fighting with each other to take reign. My happiness and logic were fighting with each other.

'Hey, is everything ok?' Mark came to me and wrapped his arms around me from the back.

'Yeah, everything's fine. Let's go, mister caring,' I said smirking.

We held hands and started walking around. Everything was so beautiful. A life I had only dreamt of, read in books about was becoming true. I was happy, the happiest I have ever been in my shitty life.

'So, what now?' I asked Mark.

'What do you mean?'

'What about us, I mean who are we?'

'Who do you want us to be, Miss, wanna date me?'

I started blushing and tried to hide my face.

'Hey, you blushing? Show me, show me.' He tried to look at my face, and I kept hiding it.

'If you want to do that then I'm going.' I said and started walking away.

'Would u like to be my girlfriend?' He shouted.

When I turned to him, he was kneeling on one foot smiling. Though it was an extremely cliché and cheesy gesture, I felt happy. I had no words to describe it. Before I could even speak, tears rushed down my eyes. Mark got up and came to me. I hugged him tightly and kept crying with happiness in his arms.

'So did you make up with James?' I asked rubbing my eyes.

'Whose James?' He asked.

I looked into his eyes, and it felt like he had no idea. I was still. I couldn't speak, I couldn't think. I didn't know what was happening.

'Hey, are you ok?' Mark asked with a worried look on his face.

'Oh, never mind. I was confusing my dream with reality.' I said smiling so as to not let him be apprehensive.

'Would you mind telling me your dream girlfriend?' He asked.

'Sure, let's go to a nice restaurant and I'll tell you all about it, boyfriend.' I said smiling but inside I was scared.

Chapter Twenty Three
REALITY

I was terrified. I didn't know what to do. On the one hand, I was trying to convince myself that he must've forgotten about him but on the other, it was like I knew something was wrong. Everything was happening as I'd imagined, the way I imagined. It felt too good to be true and I was starting to believe it was too good to be true. If it was an illusion or delusion or fake, then where was I. What was this place that I was in? I had a million questions and zero answers. I was spiralling, my mind was spiralling. I just wanted a way out, I just needed a way out, but I also wanted that happiness that was right in front of me.

At that time when I went out of the spacecraft, I was ready to sacrifice myself so everyone else could live. I was afraid of death while I made the decision, I was afraid when I was enacting it, but I was smiling thinking about what could've been. A life I could've had if everything had been okay. Now there I was, not even sure what reality is anymore, stuck in this labyrinth.

***

I was spending every day and night thinking about what was wrong, about where I was. I had to put on a fake smile, a mask when in front of others, in front of Mark. But somehow, that smile and mask had become the real me. It felt like I was ready to accept everything the way it was. I was very happy with everything. Me with Mark, us together enjoying life. But I didn't even know if he was the real Mark. I was happy and sad at the same time. I couldn't explain the feeling, but it was not nice. I had started looking forward to my fake day with fake people. I wasn't sure what was true or what was fake anymore. What existed and what didn't.

I had been thinking and rethinking about each and everything. I had read a lot of stuff, and made a lot of theories about the situation I was in. I was very confused about everything. Nothing made proper sense, but the one thing I was sure about was that I was in a labyrinth and each labyrinth has a loophole, and I had to find one.

Chapter Twenty Four
PERFECTLY IMPERFECT

1 year later

We moved in together, Mark asked me and I oh so happily said yes. I was so excited the moment he asked me, I just couldn't think about anything else. Mark was just perfect and we'd been leaving a near-perfect life. He made me feel so pretty and happy. He was like a girl's dream boyfriend. I was so happy that it couldn't be explained in words.

I still used to think about how all of it was not real while lying in bed at night. The thoughts just came to my mind, and they made me feel sad, but the happiness was so much more than the sadness could ever be, so I didn't do much about it.

3 years later

Mark proposed to me. Marcus Robinson proposed to me. He went down on one knee and proposed to me. There were puppies all around (He knows I love them), he sang a song by my favourite singer, took me out to dinner and gave me the most beautiful ring ever.

There's no way I could have said no. There's no fucking way, I could have said no to the love of my life, to my soulmate. We were gonna get married and I was thrilled.

5 Years Later

We were living an extremely joyous and happy life. Everything was just perfect. We got two dogs, and two gorgeous huskies. We had a nice house; a great neighbourhood and I was very happy with my current dream-like life.

I was laying in our bed, playing with Coco and Coso (our dogs). Mark came into the room and slowly laid down beside me facing the other direction while playing with Coco.

'How was your day, Jaze?' He asked in a sweet yet teasing voice.

'I told you not to call me that!' I said in a tone implying some anger but also showing a playful mood. 'It was great though; I had a lot of fun today. I even went shopping with my besties, I bought something for you too, do u wanna look at it?'

'Umm, sure but first I need to tell u something,' he said while getting up and sitting on the bed. Then tapping the mattress signalling me to sit beside him and I followed his command.

The joyful atmosphere had been lost in the room. Mark seemed to be in a really bad state of mind which was increasing my heart rate rapidly. I decided to stay calm, pushing away the negative thoughts which were trying to reach my brain, and asked him, 'What's up, Markey?'

He smiled a bit, but his mood showed no signs of changing. 'How'd you think of this super unique name Jazey.' He said with a smile, but I was pretty sure it was forced.

I held one of his hands in my hands clasping it tightly and asked, 'What's the matter, Mark? Don't try to avoid the topic, tell me what's bothering you.' Just as I finished saying it, his smile disappeared.

'I am sick, Jaz.' Just as he completed saying those words, water started coming out of my eyes.

My brain was unable to comprehend it. Maybe it's just a normal problem, it's probably nothing to worry about, he must be playing a prank on me, were the thoughts clouding my head.

'You're joking, right? Come on Mark. You know I don't like these jokes.' His expression still didn't change.

'It's treatable, right? You will be back to normal in no time, right?'

'No Jaz, I will not be fine. It's a new virus, and I am the first one to contract it.' He smiled a bit. 'Sounds so cool right. I have become the first person on Earth to contract a virus. I must be something special.' The smile slowly disappears, 'The doctors say that I must have contracted in space. I don't know how the fuck you can contract a virus on space. Did it have to be me Jaz. Why do I have to die? WHY! WHAT DID I DO TO DESERVE THIS!' He said as tears came rushing down his face and he broke down crying.

I hugged him and he hugged back with both of us crying together.

5 Years and 6 Months Later

I thought I could handle it, I thought I could live without him, but I can't. I am standing here at his funeral with no one to comfort me, cause the only family I had, the only person who could comfort me and ever get me through those tough times had disappeared from this world. What remained was his dead body.

As I was seeing him lay dead in a casket, the past came rushing back in.

'This is not even real right! He is not real. He wasn't even real, to begin with. Everything here is not real. I am not even in the reality. This is a paradox. I was supposed to solve it. How could I forget about it? He is alive in the real world. I need to go back to him. Yes, I should go back to him. He must have been missing me…'

I had gone completely crazy. I didn't know what was what. My mind was spiralling like never before. I just wanted to get out of this, like just wake up like it was a dream. I went to the nearest building as fast as I could, ran to the terrace and decided to jump from it. I know I sound insane. But I thought if this is not real then maybe dying could take me back. I leaped forward and jumped.

Chapter Twenty Five

IN BETWEEN

I thought that something would happen. The moment I jumped; something would happen. But it didn't. I found myself at the same place I was when I first entered this labyrinth. 5 years and 6 months ago, when I was in the hospital…

The moment I opened my eyes, I got up and opened the hospital room window, and jumped again. I didn't die. Came back to the same place again.

I kept on doing the same thing repeatedly in hope of something happening, but it didn't. Before I must have sounded crazy, but at that moment I had gone insane.

I had forgotten about going back, rather I just wanted to die. I was killing myself to have some peace. I just wanted to escape.

It had already been about 100 times that I had killed myself and ended up in the same damn place again. Feeling that excruciating pain one feels when one dies over and over again had completely broken me.

After killing myself yet another time, I was laying in the hospital bed having given up on living and dying. I closed my eyes and decided to sleep in hope of getting at least a little bit of rest, a little bit of comfort.

THE END

SPACECRAFT
DIARIES

1

'No, he has to come. Please you can't leave him behind. He is my family.' A young girl who was supposedly around 15 or 16 said to one of the officials appointed for deciding who was to be taken as a resident in the spacecraft. She kneeled unable to stand, crying, trembling, tears dripping down through the end of her nose and shouting from the top of her voice. She was unable to hold herself together.

'Oh dear, It's okay. I am probably going to die within a year. I am sure these people know what they are doing and I am sure you will be just fine without me.' An old man said picking up the girl from the floor.

'Grandpa, no. I am not going to let these people leave you behind. You still have a few years left with us. I can't leave you. I want you to come with us too.'

'Sorry ma'am, but the list has already been decided and nothing else can be done.' The official said.

The girl cried latching onto her grandpa. 'You will be just fine, Bella. Don't worry.' The girl's grandpa said trying to console her.

The spacecrafts were to be launched that very day. So, there wasn't much time left and the boarding had already started. The girl wasn't moving from her place, even though her mother was trying to get her to go.

Then she saw the lead team for the main spacecraft getting in and suddenly got up with all her might and ran towards them.

'Dr. Robinson,' She shouted. But he didn't answer her. She shouted everybody's names, they looked at her for a bit but didn't pay much attention. Everybody seemed completely worn out. They were all surrounded by security so she wasn't able to get close to them. She shouted and shouted until they ultimately went in paying her no mind.

Then came the last call for passengers to come in. Nobody was able to get her to go in the spacecraft. So, one of the security members held her and took her into the spacecraft as the door closed. She tried to get out of his hands but due to the strength difference, wasn't able to. At last, the spacecrafts ultimately took off and the girl's grandpa was left on earth to die much sooner than anticipated.

2

A few hundred metres afar from where the girl was crying, another gorgeous-looking blonde girl, Sarah, was being proposed to by a black-haired American guy, Jim.

Jim and Sarah had been together for 7 years, living a lovely life filled with laughter, been through thick and thin, and still loved each other with their whole heart.

'I have never seen such a beautiful girl like you. The moment I first saw you, I couldn't believe my eyes, that I was seeing such a beauty, that such a beauty even existed.' Jim said while kneeling down on one knee with a ring box in his hand. 'I love how you are so honest, clingy, and get jealous easily. How you get dramatic over small things. How you do small things for me which you may think I do not notice but honestly, I do. I love every single part of you Sarah, and I can't imagine living my life with anyone else except the most beautiful woman in the world, who stands right in front of me.' Sarah's eyes were filled with tears of happiness. Before Jim could finally ask her to marry him, 'YES, YES, YES, YES, YES, YES, YES, YESSSSSS…' Sarah said. They both hugged each other not letting go, filled with happiness.

***

They were residents of spacecraft no. 23 and boarded it right after the proposal. They both decided that they couldn't wait any longer and wanted to be married as soon as possible. That was probably going to be the first-ever marriage on the spacecraft. The staff was asked to make all the preparations and they were happy to oblige.

Soon the launch was made. They decided to get married before the collision of the black holes. The wedding was arranged very fast, but for them, it was the most beautiful day of their lives. They got married and were both in absolute joy. The marriage was also broadcasted on every spacecraft.

But then the collision happened and getting lost in space happened. Nothing was as simple as it seemed. The spacecraft had been transported to somewhere entirely different. The planets looked like fireballs. Before they could do anything red creatures with fire for their heads and an unusual body came inside the spacecraft by creating a hole on top of it. They spoke an entirely different language and nobody could understand what they said. In a matter of seconds, they started killing everyone. The whole spacecraft was being destroyed.

Jim and Sarah had a room a lot further than where the creatures had landed and as soon as they got to know about the creatures, they were both terrified and didn't know what to do. Neither one was able to console the other. Both of them were holding on to each other and trembling out of fear.

It was confirmed that they both were going to die but none of them wanted to speak the words. Jim picked up the death tablet which had popped out as it was supposed to in case of an attack to escape a painful death. Sarah seemed to understand what he wanted to do and nodded. They both hugged each other tightly and then Jim opened his mouth and put the pill on his tongue and kissed Sarah. Everyone on the spacecraft 23 was killed with no one left.

Jim and Sarah did die but they died together. With their lips enveloped in each other even at the end.

Acknowledgement

I am so glad that I was able to write and get this book published. But it would not have been possible without a few people which is why I would like to give them my sincere thanks and gratitude.

Firstly, I would like to thank my mom Pooja Malhotra and my dad Vedant Malhotra for making my dream come true by getting this book published. Evincepub (Publisher), for assisting me throughout the whole journey. Then my cousins, Manan Wadhawan, Hardik Dhawan, Navya Kapoor for reading, reviewing, and offering suggestions on my work. I would also like to thank my friends (You know who you are), Pranjal Aggarwal, Pranveer Singh, Theane, etc. who helped me a lot too.

Lastly, I would also like to thank Gungun Panchal for the beautiful Illustration for Part 2 of the novel.

They always helped me keep my focus and encouraged me when I felt down. I wouldn't have been able to complete it without them.

NOTE FROM THE AUTHOR

Thank you for taking the time to read my novel. I hope you liked it. I would be really glad if you could go and write your honest review about this on Amazon or Flipkart or Kobo or Goodreads. Anywhere you feel comfortable.

THANK YOU, SOO MUCH

Hope to see you again.